D1015654

# Brinley Discovers Santa

## A Bold Introduction to the Meaning Behind Santa Claus

# Brinley Discovers Santa

## A Bold Introduction to the Meaning Behind Santa Claus

Written By
## Brooke Smith

Illustrated By
## Robbie Myers

tate publishing
CHILDREN'S DIVISION

Published by Tate Publishing & Enterprises, LLC
127 E. Trade Center Terrace | Mustang, Oklahoma 73064 USA
1.888.361.9473 | www.tatepublishing.com

Tate Publishing is committed to excellence in the publishing industry. The company reflects the philosophy established by the founders, based on Psalm 68:11,
*"The Lord gave the word and great was the company of those who published it."*

Published in the United States of America
ISBN: 978-1-68270-732-6
1. Juvenile Fiction / General
2. Juvenile Fiction / Social Issues / Values & Virtues
15.05.22

Written to help you go slow and to grow,
but don't grow too slow.

For Tierzah who follows this rule,
Warren who just won't,
and Nicholas who always has.

You three are the wisest people I know.

To Robbie for inviting me to the wedding (not yours…),
and stopping everything to make this dream a success;
proving there are miracles in taking a chance.

Finally, to Jeff. For giving love. The best thing to give.
Brooke, Mo.M.

---

Robbie Myers wants to dedicate this book to the odd way
life can be & to those who struggle.
Never give up hope.

And to Brooke, for believing in me and trusting that I
could be a part in making her dreams come true.

Most importantly, to Braddah (and your best
friends, Emma & Walter),  for sacrificing
many adventures so I could find my way home.

I was riding home on the bus with my best friend Randi. We were excited because it was the last day of school before winter break. Randi was telling me all about what she was going to do during her vacation. She said she wanted to go sledding with her family and they're going to have her cousins and aunts and uncles over for dinner on Christmas Eve. She was bouncing on the seat, she was so excited. Randi can be silly sometimes, and she makes me laugh so hard!

I asked what Randi wanted for Christmas. She sat up on her knees and said, *"I'm gonna ask Santa for a skateboard!"*

Just then the bus went quiet. I looked around, and everyone was looking at us.

This kid, Mark started laughing and pointing his finger at us from the back of the bus. Mark always sits at the back of the bus, and if you try to sit in that seat he'll yell at you!

I don't know for sure, but I think Mark has to be in fifth grade. But he looks even bigger than that. Mark is never nice. One time he pushed me when I was standing in line to get on the bus and he stole my spot in line. I don't know why he does stuff like that, and I don't know why he never gets in trouble either. But he always gets away with it.

Then, Mark stood up and started walking toward us on the bus. You aren't supposed to walk on the bus while it's moving. But I wasn't gonna tell on him.

Mark stopped at our seat and sat down. I got squished between the wall of the bus and Randi. Then Mark looked at us and said, "It was the two of you talking about Santa Claus, wasn't it?"

He said 'Santa Claus' in a mean way that made me feel bad, but I didn't know why.

Then, I couldn't believe it!

Randi stood up and got right in Mark's
face and said,

*"Yeah we're talking about Santa, and we know what he's
gonna bring you for Christmas,
a big lump of coal!"*

Randi sat down and looked out the window.

Mark started laughing really hard after that. He had his head thrown back and his fist was punching on his knee. He even had his leg stretching into the aisle of the bus kicking!

But then he stopped laughing and he looked at me and then he looked at Randi and he said,

**"I hate to break it to you, but there is no Santa, kids. Your folks have been lyin' to ya. Merry Christmas!"**

Then he got up and went to his seat at the back of the bus.

I was so *scared*
and *sad*
that I thought I was
going to *cry*.

I didn't say one more
word for the rest
of the ride home.

Randi didn't either.

When I got home, I felt **mad**.

I was **mad** at Mark for saying those
mean things about Santa.

I was **mad** at Randi for telling Mark that he was getting
coal for Christmas.

I slammed the front door when I got into my house and
I ran to find my mom.

Mom was in the kitchen with my little sister, Kelsey, making cookies. They were chocolate chip cookies, but they were in the shape of Christmas trees! I reached for one, but then my mom said, "No, no, honey. Those cookies aren't for you."

# Then I got **mad** at my mom.

I ran to my room and I slammed my door shut as hard as I could. I couldn't believe it. Now I was **mad** at Mark and Randi and even my mom!

When I got up this morning, I thought it was going to be a fun day. It was our last day of school before winter break. Two whole weeks with no school! But today was **NOT** fun.

And then I thought of something. What if Mark was right? What if there is no Santa and what if Mom and Dad have been lying to me all this time?

I was so **mad** and *sad*, and I felt *lonely* too. My mom wasn't coming to check on me. She didn't even ask me how my day was. Now I'm hungry, too.

I started to *cry* really hard.

I hugged my favorite pillow.

It's the pillow that Grammy got for me
last time she visited.

*That was a long time ago.*

*I miss Grammy.*

I guess I fell asleep, 'cause when I woke up it was dark outside. I could smell the cookies coming from the kitchen.

I got up and went to the kitchen. I saw Kelsey and Mom there, so I sat down at the counter. I was still really *sad* about what Mark said about Santa and I was **mad** about not getting a cookie when I got home.

Mom and Kelsey were wrapping up the cookies on paper plates with pretty green tissue paper and red ribbons and gift cards.

"What are those for, anyway, and why are you making them so pretty?" I asked.

My mom never even looked at me while she was wrapping the cookies up, and Kelsey was holding the ribbons so mom could tie them up in a bow. Mom said, "These are to surprise our neighbors, honey. Isn't that a great idea? We get to play Santa!"

I didn't think this was a great idea. What did she mean, 'we get to play Santa?' Does that mean Mark was wrong about Santa? Thinking about Mark just made me feel sick to my stomach, and I couldn't help but say, "Why would we want to give strangers cookies? And anyway, **there is no Santa, haven't you heard?**"

I was hoping to get Mom's attention when I said that.

It worked.

Kelsey looked at me like she was going to cry. Mom looked at Kelsey and told her that I was wrong about Santa. She helped Kelsey down from the counter and asked her to go to her room so she could talk to me. Then she told Kelsey, "When Brinley and I are done talking we'll finish our Santa project. And who knows, maybe Brinley will help out too!"

I looked at them both and said,
**"I won't help out because
I actually exist!"**

It didn't make me feel good to say that. But I was **mad!** I don't know why Mark said those mean things to me on the bus. I don't know why I couldn't have a cookie when I got home from school. I *missed* my grammy. And Mom was talking about Santa like he was in the same room with us! I don't know what to think about anyone, and I feel like being mean to everyone.

When Kelsey left the kitchen, Mom picked up a cookie and handed it to me. She sat down next to me at the kitchen table. I took the cookie, but I didn't feel like eating it.

"Who told you Santa Claus isn't real?" Mom asked with a worried sounding voice.

Her worried voice made me think for a second. Then I said, "*Everyone knows it, Mom. Why have you lied to me my whole life?*" I almost had to whisper when I said this because there was a big lump in my throat like I was going to cry. I wanted to be tough for this talk. Only big kids have talks that are this serious, and big kids don't cry, right?

Mom put her arms around me and hugged me.

Then she picked me up and put me on her lap. It felt really good to be hugged.

Mom got really serious, and talked in a sweet voice.

She said, "You're not right about this, Brinley. I know that a lot of people don't believe in Santa Claus, but I do. And your father does. Santa is real. You are right that the Santa we see in the mall isn't the real one. And you're even right to think that the idea of Santa being a big, jolly man in a red suit with a fluffy, white beard, who twitches his nose and is able to come into your house through your chimney isn't correct. That idea is the best way grown-ups know how to explain the real Santa to little kids. Brinley, only big kids and adults can know what I am about to tell you. Are you ready to hear this?"

I nodded my head. I couldn't stand to look mom in the face, so I just kept looking at my cookie.

"Brinley, Santa Claus is the spirit of Christmas. But more than that, sweetheart, and this is the most important part, Santa is the spirit of giving. Santa is the feeling you get when you do good things for people. Santa is inside of you and me and daddy and Kelsey and Grammy. Remember the pillow that Grammy got for you? Your favorite pillow that you sleep with every night is a part of Santa because Grammy gave that to you to help you feel good when you hug it. Also that pillow helps you remember Grammy.

All of these feelings are good feelings,
and all of these good feelings
are a part of Santa Claus and they come from
the spirit of giving."

Mom stopped talking for a minute. And I thought about what she said. I had a lot of questions still. Mom started talking before I could even start to ask my questions, but I didn't interrupt because I hoped she would tell me more about Santa.

She said, "The cookies that Kelsey and I are wrapping up so pretty are an important part of Christmas, too. And they are an important part of every day. When we give those cookies to people who aren't expecting them, my hope is that those people decide to do something nice for someone else, too. I hope that the cookies help them feel good and they can turn around and help someone else feel good. By giving out these cookies, we are being Santa's elves. I'd like you to be an elf too. Will you help us finish the cookies?"

I didn't know what to think about Santa, but I wanted to be with Mom and Kelsey and so I did want to help out. *"Yeah, I'll help you,"* I said in a whisper.

"Great," Mom said!  Then she looked at my face and placed a kiss on my forehead and said, "Have you read the gift cards yet?"

"No," I said.

Mom handed me a card and we read it together. It said,

These cookies were made by two little elves who are learning about the spirit of Santa.
Please enjoy these treats with your family and have a very happy holiday season.

These cookies were made by two little elves who are learning about the spirit of Santa. Please enjoy these treats with your family and have a very happy holiday season.

I thought the card was nice. They made me feel a little better just to read them.

Before mom got Kelsey from her room, she looked at me and said, "Just watch how this project makes you feel, honey. I promise you that it feels really good to reach out in this way." Then she went to find Kelsey.

Kelsey looked *sad* when she came back to the kitchen. She came right to me and asked me, "Did you really mean that there is no Santa Claus? Mom said we are helping Santa with the cookies. Mom said we were being Santa's elves."

I looked into Kelsey's *sad* eyes. I was *sad* that I made her feel *bad* about Santa. I held her hand and told her, "Mom talked to me and explained Santa to me. I'm *sorry* that I was **mad**, Kelsey. I got my feelings hurt by some kid on the bus, but Mom is right, and Santa is real. The kid on the bus said Santa's not real, and he teased me because I believe in him. I guess he doesn't understand about Santa. I didn't either. But Mom told me all about Santa, and now I know that Santa is real, and he lives inside of you and me. What you are doing with Mom is what I'm gonna call a Santa Act! Can you teach me to be an elf too, Kelsey?"

Me

You

Santa Acts

Kelsey was so excited to teach me about being an elf that she started jumping up and down. "Yeah, I'll teach you! It's so fun! You won't believe it. We'll drop off the cookies at our neighbors' houses and just leave them there. We aren't even gonna tell them we brought them. It will be like a big surprise. Just like on Christmas morning when we get to open presents!"

Just seeing how excited Kelsey was helped me feel better. I jumped out of my chair and sat up at the kitchen counter to help Mom and Kelsey finish wrapping up Santa's elves' cookies. My job was to put the cards on top of the tissue paper. It was a very important job, indeed!

I still feel *sad* sometimes that there isn't a fat man in a red suit with flying reindeer. But now I can see that Santa is the most **exciting** way that Mom and Dad have to teach me about the spirit of giving during Christmas time. And besides, pretending that Santa is coming to our house on Christmas Eve **is** really fun. And now that I'm a big kid, Mom and Dad said that I get to help lay out all of the presents that Santa's going to leave on Christmas Eve. I know now that helping people feel good is what Santa is all about.

Playing Santa reminds me of other times that I've helped out, too. Like when I give my old coats to the thrift store downtown, or when we visit the animals at the Humane Society, or even when we leave a can of corn in the box on our way out of the grocery store for the homeless shelter. Now I understand why Mom says it makes her feel good to put cans in that box. It makes me feel good when I do things to help other people, too. And Christmas time is the best time to play along!

Since I learned about Santa Claus, I made a secret promise to myself to do something special for someone every year. I will try to do things to help people feel good every time I remember to.

*I will make my own Santa Acts every day!*

The End